Samantha Smartypants
and the
Slippery Slope

To Hillside Library,
If you really want something
badly enough, you can do it!
Barbara Puccia

Samantha Smartypants
and the
Slippery Slope

by Barbara Puccia
Illustrated by Emma Kane

ISBN-13:978-1515200390
ISBN-10:1515200396

Summary: When Ms. Thompson hands out discount flyers for Devil's Drop ski resort, Samantha starts to panic. Sliding around on all that snow sounds way too dangerous. The popular kids already know how to ski and the kids in her lesson never seem to fall. Then, to make matters worse, there's a new girl in class who challenges Samantha in a whole different way. Will Samantha make it down the slippery slope or will she wipe out trying?

Contents

CHAPTER 1

DEVIL'S DROP

Ms. Thompson's eyes got so bright, it looked like she swallowed a light bulb.

"Boys and girls," she said to our third grade class. "Guess what I have?" She held up some colorful flyers. On the front of them, I saw pictures of people skiing.

"Ooh, I love to ski," said Lisa Logan. "I got a brand new ski outfit for my birthday. It's so cool." Her best friend, Deena Jackson, nodded.

1

"I don't ski. I snowboard," said Bobby Stanger. "I bet I can beat the whole class racing down the mountain!" He gave his best friend, Tommy Tagaloney, a fist bump.

I never skied or snowboarded before so I didn't say anything. My one and only friend, Peter Cavelli, just shrugged. He probably never skied either. Sliding around on all that snow sounded just like a recipe for disaster. Which didn't mean it sounded like cooking instructions for a terrible meal. It just meant I'd probably fall and hurt myself.

"I have discount flyers for Devil's Drop ski resort for the winter holiday," said Ms. Thompson. "I'll hand them out to bring home to your parents."

Devil's Drop, I thought. Who would want to ski at a place called that?

"What's a discount?" asked Lisa.

"That's when you get something for less money than the normal price," I said.

"Samantha Smartypants!" said Bobby.

That's not my real name. It's really Samantha Pojanowski. Some kids call me Samantha Smartypants instead. That's because back in September, Bobby got mad when I got 100 on all my tests and answered all Ms. Thompson's questions. He called me Smartypants and soon everyone caught on. Well, everyone except for Peter. At first, it bothered me, but now I just ignore it.

"Well," said Ms. Thompson. "Devil's Drop is offering discounts on ski and snowboard rentals for the holidays. And lessons too."

"I don't need lessons," said Bobby. "I'm already a pro."

"Me neither," said Tommy.

"Maybe my mom will buy me new designer goggles," said Lisa.

"Or new pink ski mittens," said Deena.

Then, Ms. Thompson told us all about how she learned to ski when she was in second grade. She went skiing with her family every year. She loved it so much she even went to Switzerland.

Going to Switzerland sounded like fun, but skiing was way too scary. I didn't want to try it even if we saved a thousand bucks in discounts.

Ms. Thompson handed out the flyers and waited for us to put them in our homework folders.

"Okay," said Ms. Thompson. "Please take out your spelling boots."

Everyone giggled.

"Books," I said out loud.

But Ms. Thompson had this far away look in her eyes like she was still on some mountain in Switzerland. I don't think she even heard me.

CHAPTER 2

FOUND OUT

When I got home from school, my mom asked how the day went. I decided not to tell her about the ski flyer.

After a snack, I went to my room to do homework. I whizzed through the math and spelling, and read a chapter in my history book. It didn't take long because homework was easy for me. On the other hand, skiing at Devil's Drop seemed like the hardest job in the universe.

After a while, my mom knocked on my door. She always knocked even though I kept the door open. That's because one time I was so busy reading, I didn't even see her standing there calling my name.

"Hey Samantha. I just got a call from Peter's mom," she said. "Mrs. Cavelli wondered if we got the flyer for Devil's Drop. The one Ms. Thompson gave out in class."

"Oh," I said. "Maybe I lost it. Or maybe Ms. Thompson forgot to give me one." I knew that wasn't exactly true, but because I said maybe, it wasn't a lie either.

"Let's just check your homework folder," she said. My mom could be pretty smart sometimes. She found the flyer and read it.

"Wow. This looks like fun. There's discounts on motels and restaurants too. What do you think Samantha?"

"Oh no. It doesn't look like such a great deal to me. We could go to the library and get books for free instead of spending all that money." I loved books and my mom knew it.

"Yes, but we can go to the library anytime. This deal is only for the holidays."

I knew I had to figure out something fast to discourage my mom. Once she got an idea in her head, it stuck like glue.

"I used to ski a lot when I was younger," said my mom. "I learned when I was just about your age."

Uh, oh, I thought. Here we go again. I wondered if my mom had skied in Switzerland with Ms. Thompson.

"Well, we'll discuss it with your dad when he gets home. Think about it, Samantha. It might be fun."

Right then and there, I knew I had to come up with a plan so we didn't go skiing. Maybe I could pretend I twisted my ankle. Or fake a fever. I'd have to think fast to get the idea unstuck from my mom's head. Thinking about it made my body shake like a bowl of jell-o on a roller coaster ride.

7

When my dad got home, my mom told him all about Devil's Drop.

"What a great idea," he said. "I started skiing when I was seven."

Oh no, I thought. I was outnumbered. I guessed I was going to Devil's Drop after all.

That night I had a nightmare. I lay in a hospital bed and the doctor came in to talk to my parents about my ski accident. The doctor had a red cape around his shoulders, horns on his head, and a pitchfork in his hand. Yikes. So did my mom and dad!

CHAPTER 3

PIZZA AND FRENCH FRIES

At school the next day, all the kids talked about the ski trip. The buzz in the room got so loud, it sounded like the time my dad stepped on a beehive and all the bees went crazy.

"My mom said we can go skiing and stay overnight," said Lisa, beaming like a glow stick.

"Me too," said Deena. "I can't wait."

"I'm gonna snowboard on No Return," said Bobby.

"No Return," said Lisa. "That's what the sales lady told my mom when she tried to return a purse that didn't match her dress."

"No Return's the name of a ski run," I said. I'd looked up the ski resort on the Internet the night before.

"Smartypants!" said Lisa. I ignored her.

"Our families are gonna meet at the mountain and ski together," Peter said to me. "It'll be fun."

He looked excited. I guessed Peter wasn't scared like me.

Later that day, Ms. Thompson took us to the library, my favorite place in the whole school. If I could spend all day there, every day, I'd be the happiest person in the universe.

"Do you have any books that teach you how to ski?" I asked Mrs. Bookbinder, the librarian.

"Let's look," she said.

We searched the computer catalog, and sure enough, we found a book for beginners.

I grabbed it from the shelf and started reading. This is what it said:

The most important thing to learn when skiing is how to slow down and stop.

That sounded like good advice.

Make a pizza with your skis.

It showed a picture of someone on skis. The front tips of his skis touched while the backs were wide apart, making it look like a slice of pizza.

When you get better at skiing, make French fries with your skis.

Now the person had their skis side by side like two French fries. Suddenly, my stomach started growling. I loved pizza and French fries, even if my mom said French fries weren't healthy. I got so hungry, I kept thinking about food instead of skiing. Maybe learning to ski from a book wasn't the best idea after all!

CHAPTER 4

NEW KID

After library, we returned to our classroom. I saw Ms. Thompson, a girl in a wheelchair, and a lady with a huge smile at the front of the room.

"That's the new kid," Lisa whispered.

"Why's she in a wheelchair?" asked Deena.

"She probably had an accident," said Bobby.

Ms. Thompson told us to take our seats. "We have a new student joining our class. I want you to welcome Sophia Lin."

Everyone stared at Sophia. I knew it wasn't polite, but it was hard not to stare because her head tilted to one side and drool came out the side of her mouth. She held one arm at a weird angle.

"And this is Mrs. Sparkle," said Ms. Thompson, pointing to the smiley lady. "She'll be helping Sophia out."

"Hi class," said Mrs. Sparkle, still smiling.

Peter raised his hand.

"Yes, Peter," said Ms. Thompson.

"As class president, I want to welcome Sophia to our class. Hi Sophia," he said. "My name is Peter." Peter always seemed to know what to do and say.

"Thank you, Peter," said Ms. Thompson.

Sophia said something but I couldn't understand her words.

That's when I realized I was class president, too. Peter and I got the same amount of votes during our class election. Ms. Thompson called us co-presidents. I raised my hand.

"Yes, Samantha," said Ms. Thompson.

"I want to welcome Sophia, too. Hi. I'm Samantha."

"H..iii," Sophia said. But it sounded strange, kind of muffled.

Everybody quieted down.

Ms. Thompson asked three kids to move their chairs over to make space.

"You can come here," she said to Sophia.

Sophia pushed a lever on her wheelchair and presto, she scooted right over to Ms. Thompson. Then she pushed the lever to one side and her wheelchair spun around so fast I did a double-take. Which didn't mean I took two pictures with a camera. It just meant I got surprised. Sophia faced the front of the classroom just like that.

"Wow!" said Bobby to Tommy. "We should get us some wheelchairs."

"What for?" asked Tommy.

"So we can race them at recess," said Bobby. "I wonder how fast they go."

"Shhh," said Ms. Thompson. She handed Mrs. Sparkle a math book.

"Okay," she said. "Let's turn to page 23."

Everybody pretended to stop staring and look at their books, but I could see they still snuck looks at Sophia out of the corners of their eyes.

Mrs. Sparkle sat down next to Sophia. She placed a tray on the arms of her wheelchair and clicked it in place. Next, she opened the math book and set it on the tray. Sophia lifted her left arm and dropped it on the book. Mrs. Sparkle tilted Sophia's head down so that she focused right at page 23.

I wondered what kind of accident made Sophia need all that help. I bet it was skiing. Good thing I didn't need help like that. I liked to do things all by myself!

CHAPTER 5

A NEW SMARTYPANTS

The next day, Ms. Thompson gave us our weekly spelling test.

"Number one...*cloud*," she said. "There's not a *cloud* in the sky."

We wrote *cloud* on a piece of paper.

"Look," whispered Bobby to Tommy. "Sophia's cheating. She's using a laptop to look up the words."

I turned to Sophia. She stared at a laptop on her tray. I knew she wasn't cheating, but I didn't want to say anything during the test.

"Quiet," said Ms. Thompson. "Eyes up front."

"Number two...*wrong,*" she said. "The paint is the *wrong* color."

"It's *wrong* to cheat," whispered Lisa. She snuck a peek at Sophia.

"Shhh," said Ms. Thompson. "The next person who talks gets an F."

Everybody got real quiet after that.

We finished the test and went to lunch. I sat down with Peter. We heard kids talking at the end of the table.

"That girl Sophia had a really bad accident," said Deena.

"She wasn't in an accident," I said. "She has cerebral palsy."

The night before, my mom told me that. She said Sophia's family had just moved into the house down the street.

"Terrible palsy?" said Lisa. "Well, she sure looks terrible. Did you see her drooling? And her left arm is all crooked."

"No," I said. "Cerebral...not terrible." Lisa probably mixed up the words because they rhymed.

"Well, whatever she has, she shouldn't have cheated," said Deena. "I could have looked up the words on my laptop, too."

"She wasn't cheating," I said. "Sophia's brain got damaged at birth. It has trouble telling her body how to move, which is why her face and legs droop and her left arm is crooked. She has trouble writing and speaking too. It's easier for her to type than write. That's why she uses a laptop."

"Smartypants!" said Bobby.

Here we go again, I thought. My mom and I had looked up cerebral palsy on the Internet and that's how I found out all about it.

"Well, I'd rather have a tank top than a laptop anyway," said Lisa.

"Me too," said Deena, giggling.

They both wore bright pink tank tops underneath their sweaters. I bet their parents spent millions of dollars getting them the most popular clothes at the mall.

"Well, if her brain got damaged, then she must be dumb," said Bobby. "I bet I get a better grade than her on the spelling test."

That wasn't going to happen. Bobby usually got the lowest grade in class and this time probably wouldn't be any different.

"Whatever," said Lisa. "Why is Sophia in our class anyway? She should be in a special class for kids like her. She can't write or move or speak very well. And worst of all, she can't have sleepovers or go shopping."

"Or dance, or paint," said Deena.

"Or play sports," said Bobby.

I didn't really care that she couldn't do all those things. I didn't like most of those things anyway. Maybe Sophia liked to read books or look things up on the Internet like me. Maybe I could even make friends with Sophia.

Back in class after lunch, Ms. Thompson handed us back our spelling tests. She said one student got 100. I looked at my paper. On the top, it said *100* and the words *Great job, Samantha!* in bright red ink.

Then Ms. Thompson surprised us all.

"And guess what," she said. "One student got 110 on her test."

Wow, I thought. That meant someone got all the words right and the bonus word for extra credit. Nobody ever did that. Not even Peter, or me.

"Great job, Sophia," said Ms. Thompson, smiling. "I think we have an expert speller in our class."

"No way!" said Bobby.

Bobby looked at Sophia. Then he looked at me. His jaw dropped so low, I thought it might fall off his face. Then he looked back at Sophia and said, *Sophia Smartypants!* At first I thought he said *Samantha Smartypants* like he always did. But he repeated it. *Sophia Smartypants*!

Now that really took the cake. Which didn't mean that someone stole dessert. It just meant I couldn't believe it. Bobby called Sophia *Smartypants* instead of me. I never liked being teased for being smart, but I didn't like it when Sophia got a better grade than me, either. Maybe being called *Smartypants* hadn't been so bad after all!

CHAPTER 6

THE TALKING MACHINE

On Monday morning, Ms. Thompson made an announcement.

"As you know, school will be closed for the holidays. You'll be off the entire week and I'm not assigning any homework."

"Yeah!" yelled Bobby. "No homework."

"Ms. Thompson rocks!" yelled Lisa.

"Yeah," said a strange voice from the back of the classroom.

Everybody turned to look. The voice sounded just like a robot. But there were no robots in the

22

back of the classroom, only Sophia in her wheelchair.

"I thought you'd be happy about that," said Ms. Thompson."How many of you are going to spend time with your family over the holiday?"

"I am," said the robot voice.

I turned around quick as a lightning bolt to catch the robot before it disappeared again.

"My aunt and uncle and cousins are coming," the voice said.

Now that was really weird. Nobody was talking. Sophia sat in the back of the classroom with her head down, typing on an iPad. I wondered if she'd get in trouble for not paying attention.

"That's very nice, Sophia," said Ms. Thompson.

"Huh...,what?" said Bobby. "Sophia's talking?"

"Actually," said Ms. Thompson, "Sophia has an iPad with an app that helps her talk. She presses buttons with pictures, words, and letters and the app speaks for her."

"Wow," said Kevin McCann. "That's cool."

Kids craned their necks to see what Sophia was doing. I think we just wanted to hear that robot voice talk again.

"Hey, does that app have different voices?" asked Peter. He loved computers.

Sophia pressed some buttons. "Yes," answered a different voice.

"Are there any boy voices?" asked Tommy.

"I don't know," it answered.

"Does it sing or only talk?" asked Deena.

"Talk," it said.

"Can we try it?" asked Mark Klein.

"Maybe," it said.

"Okay, class," said Ms. Thompson. "I think that's enough questions for Sophia right now."

Sophia talked a lot with her machine that day. Kids kept asking her questions and she got lots of attention. Lisa didn't like that because she was used to being the most popular girl in class.

The rest of the week went by in a blur. Ms. Thompson gave us lots of schoolwork which was good because it took my mind off that scary ski trip. At least Sophia wouldn't have to go skiing, I thought. Maybe being in a wheelchair wasn't so bad after all.

CHAPTER 7

SHOPPING TRIP

Saturday morning, my mom came to my room.

"It's time to go shopping for ski clothes," she said.

I shook my head. "I have too much homework."

"You're on holiday break and Ms. Thompson didn't give you any homework. We need to get you warm clothes. Otherwise, you'll be very uncomfortable on the ski slopes."

It would take a lot more than warm clothes to make me comfortable on the slopes. Anyway, like

I said, when my mom gets an idea stuck in her head, it's impossible to get her unstuck. So off we went to the mall.

It was packed with billions of last minute holiday shoppers. Everywhere we went, we got bumped and jostled.

"First let's get you Under Armour," said my mom.

Under armor sounded just about right. Skiing was a war and I'd need armor for protection.

At the sporting goods store, a sales lady showed us racks of black tops and pants. My mom picked out two long-sleeved tops and two bottoms. We went into the dressing room and I tried them on. I had to tug to get them on, but they felt really warm. Then we shopped for ski socks with pretty colored patterns and black mittens. Finally, we looked at the ski jackets and pants. That's when my mom almost flipped her lid. Which didn't mean she tossed a pot cover over her head. It just meant she got really upset when she saw the prices. She decided to call my aunt.

"Lydia, you wouldn't happen to have any of Ellie's old ski pants and jackets?" she asked on her cell phone. "Something that might fit Samantha?" Ellie's my cousin, two years older than me.

"Uh huh, great," she said. I guessed I'd be getting hand-me-downs from Ellie.

"Can you bring them over Christmas Eve?...Great! Thank you. Bye."

"Okay, Samantha," she said. "Let's just buy these things for now. We'll get Ellie's clothes on Christmas Eve. The rest we can rent at the mountain."

"Sure," I said, thrilled to leave that crowded mall.

CHAPTER 8

HOLIDAY HAND-ME-DOWNS

On Christmas Eve, Aunt Lydia, Uncle Bill,
Ellie, and Grandpa Joe came to visit. My mom
made millions of small foods called appetizers.
The family favorite was pigs in a blanket. They
were little hot dog pieces rolled in dough and
baked in the oven. They always disappeared in the
blink of an eye. We drank eggnog and apple cider
and ate butternut squash soup, lamb, potatoes,
salad, and green bean casserole. You'd think my

mom had invited an army instead of just eight people.

After dinner, we opened presents. Aunt Lydia and Uncle Bill gave me a purple sweater with snowflakes on it.

"For your ski trip," said Aunt Lydia.

I wish she hadn't mentioned that. I dropped the sweater like a bomb about to explode.

"Oops," I said.

Then I picked it back up real fast and pretended I loved it. I didn't want to hurt anybody's feelings.

"Thank you, thank you, thank you," I said.

My mom always worried about me getting spoiled. Which didn't mean I'd been left out of the refrigerator to rot. It just meant she thought I got too many presents and wouldn't appreciate them. So just to prove I wasn't spoiled, I always said thank you at least three times for each gift.

Grandpa Joe gave me a gift card to Books and Bites. They served hot chocolate and desserts there. You could read a book while you ate without even buying the book. My mom always bought it anyway. I loved that store.

"Thank you, thank you, thank you," I said.

My parents gave me a new writing journal and the book, *Harry Potter and the Sorcerer's Stone.* I'd already read a library copy, but now I had my very own.

"Thank you, thank you, thank you."

Then, Aunt Lydia handed my mom a shopping bag stuffed like old Santa's belly. Oh no, I thought. Could it be? Sure enough, my mom pulled out Ellie's old purple jacket and black ski pants.

"Thank you, thank you, thank you," I said. But I didn't mean it, not one bit.

"I'm so jealous you're going skiing," said Ellie. "I wish I could go. I love skiing! I know you will too."

Was she crazy? I didn't say anything.

"Try on the jacket," said my mom.

I gave her an *I don't want to* look, but she made a scrunched up frown which meant I had to do it anyway.

The jacket sleeves hung below my hands, so my mom rolled them up. Other than that, it felt warm and comfy. Maybe the puffy jacket would cushion my fall when I wiped out on the mountain and rolled to the bottom.

"Now try on the pants," said my mom.

That was taking things too far. I decided to stand my ground.

"No!" I said. "I mean...I'm sure they'll fit, since the jacket did."

When my mom saw my face, she knew I'd had enough of all that ski stuff.

Soon, everybody got ready to leave. My mom made Aunt Lydia take home all the leftovers since we were going skiing the next morning. My aunt had so much food, she could have opened a supermarket.

Before bed, I made hot chocolate for Santa. I put it by the fireplace with a plate of chocolate chip cookies. That night, I tried to sleep so Santa would come, but worrying about skiing kept me awake. Then I worried that Santa wouldn't come until I fell asleep. I must have fallen asleep anyway because the next thing I knew, my parents woke me up. The day of the dreaded ski trip had arrived!

CHAPTER 9

SANTA'S SURPRISE

"Aren't you going to see if Santa came?" my mom asked.

"I can't believe you didn't get up early and run downstairs," said my dad.

"Right," I said, suddenly wide awake. I wanted to see what Santa brought but I also wanted to stay in bed and hide.

I shuffled downstairs and over to the fireplace. Sure enough, I found a cardboard box with a red bow on it. Next to the box, I saw a note. This is what it said:

Dear Samantha,

Ho Ho Ho! I hope you enjoy reading hundreds of books on your new Kindle. You can download as many as you want for vacation so your suitcase will be light as a feather. Merry Christmas!

Love, Santa Claus

"I didn't ask Santa for this," I said, turning to my parents.

"What a great idea though," said my mom. "Now you can take all those books out of your suitcase."

I'd packed four books, one for each day of vacation. I liked the feel of turning pages in real books, but I didn't want to act spoiled.

"I can still keep the *Harry Potter* book, right?" I asked.

"Of course," she said. "But you can take all the other ones out."

"Great," I said. "Santa, thank you, thank you, thank you."

I picked up the box. "I wonder how it works?"

"Let's open it." She pulled the zip strip and opened it up. Inside, we found a Kindle, a power cord, and a page of instructions.

While we read the instructions, my dad cooked breakfast. He made pancakes in the shape of Santa Claus and his reindeer. I wished he hadn't gone to all that trouble because I wasn't hungry.

"It says we have to charge the Kindle before we use it," I said, smiling. "That could take four hours. I guess we'll have to wait until it's charged before we leave."

My mom shook her head. "Nice try, Samantha. but we can charge it at the motel while we're skiing. Peter can help us download books tonight with the motel's Wi-Fi."

It seemed like my mom had been in cahoots with Santa. She had everything all worked out. I wished she hadn't mentioned Devil's Drop. It made my stomach want to drop.

"Breakfast is ready," said my Dad. "Hurry up and eat. We're leaving in half an hour."

I managed to eat Santa's hat and beard and drink my juice, but my stomach felt queasy.

"Go upstairs and get ready," said my mom. "You look a little pale."

I tried to take my time brushing my teeth and getting dressed, but my parents kept telling me to hurry. It was no use. Eventually, I trudged downstairs and sank into the car, my heart beating faster than a jackhammer.

CHAPTER 10

SUPER-SIZED

The ride to Devil's Drop only took two hours. I wished it took two million hours. My dad checked us into the motel. He said the room was ready and the Cavellis had already arrived.

"Lucky for us. We'll have plenty of time to get to the mountain for your two o'clock lesson," he said.

"Oh, right," I said, feeling like the unluckiest person in the galaxy.

He drove to Room 28 and we took all the bags out of the car. My mom let me slide the card key

38

into the lock. The first two times I tried, the red light blinked and the door stayed locked.

"Try it slower," said my mom.

Sure enough, when I slid it slower, the light changed to green and it beeped. I turned the knob and the door opened right up.

"Third time's the charm," said my Dad.

We entered a large room with two queen beds, side tables, a desk, and an armoire with a big TV inside. I saw blue bedspreads, blue curtains, and blue walls. Blue, like in black and blue, the way I'd probably be by the end of my ski lesson.

"How nice," said my mom, while my dad brought in the suitcases.

We unpacked and put our clothes in the armoire. We left our ski clothes on the bed. Then, we plugged in the Kindle to charge it.

Suddenly, we heard a knock at the door. My mom looked out of the peephole and opened it up. In walked the whole Cavelli family.

"Hi Samantha," said Peter, rushing over to me. "Guess what I got for Christmas?"

I took one look at the object in his hand and my eyes nearly popped out of my head. He had a new Kindle just like me. I wondered if Santa got a two-for-one sale at his workshop.

"I got one, too," I said. "Mine's charging up."

"I already charged mine," he said. "I'm gonna download some books."

Peter showed me how to hook up to the Wi-Fi. He said we could download books using his mom's Amazon account. We found classics like *Anne of Green Gables* and *The Secret Garden,* which I wanted, and a *Minecraft* book that Peter downloaded right then and there. We started reading the book while our parents chatted.

"Okay, kids, it's time to go," said my dad.

I looked up at Peter, but he kept reading.

"I'm scared," I said.

"Of *Minecraft*?" he asked, looking up. "But it's fun."

"No, of skiing!"

"Oh, so am I," said Peter. "But, at least we'll be in the same lesson."

The Cavellis agreed to meet us for lunch at the diner next door. They went back to their room to change.

My mom made me take my ski clothes into the bathroom to dress. The Under Armour felt snuggly warm just like in the store but when I put on Ellie's ski pants, I thought I'd taken my mom's instead. They were way too big. Even when I zipped and snapped them, they fell right to the floor. It reminded me of a clown I saw once at the circus. Every time he pulled up his pants, they fell right back down. I shuffled out to show my parents.

"Oh my," said my mom. "They're way too big. I told you to try them on yesterday."

"Well, too late now," said my dad. "What are we going to do?"

"I guess I'll have to stay in the motel while you ski," I said, suddenly feeling a whole lot better.

"Not so fast," said my mom. "I think I have a safety pin in my purse."

"Good idea," said my Dad. "See that. Every problem has a solution."

My dad always said things like that.

My mom rummaged through her purse and found a safety pin but no matter how hard she tried to pin it through the thick pants, it didn't work. The pin ended up bending instead.

I smiled. "Not gonna work."

"Well, you'll just have to wear your jeans for now," she said. "And we'll see about buying you ski pants at the mountain after your lesson."

I looked at my mom and shook my head, but she wasn't taking no for an answer. I put on my jeans, sweater, and jacket and off we went to eat.

CHAPTER 11

BOOT BOUND

We met the Cavellis at the diner and the hostess showed us to our table. Peter and I ordered grilled cheese sandwiches, but I felt too nauseous to eat. Peter wolfed his down.

"You'll do great," said Peter, grinning.

I didn't say anything.

After lunch, we piled into our cars and drove to the mountain. When we arrived, our parents bought ski passes at the ticket window with their discount coupons. We attached them to our jackets with a wire that laced through our zippers. After that, we went to another building for our rentals.

My dad filled out a whole bunch of forms. Then, a lady came over, measured my feet and brought me a pair of clunky boots. She helped me slide my toes in, but I couldn't get my heel down.

"Too tight," I said.

"Push," she said, holding the boot down while I stood up.

I pushed really hard and finally my foot went all the way in. She buckled it up with metal clasps, locking it tight. I'd have to be Harry Houdini, the magician, if I ever wanted to escape.

"Now the other one," said the lady. Could things get any worse?

When I finally got both boots on, she asked me if I could wiggle my toes.

My feet wouldn't budge but my toes moved a little. Then she asked me to walk. Was she kidding? I could barely lift them off the ground.

Every time I took a step, the boots went clunk back down.

"How do they feel?" she asked.

"Awful," I said. "They're way too heavy."

"You'll get used to them," she said. "Actually, I think they're just right."

I wondered why she even asked me.

This whole skiing thing didn't make any sense. If I couldn't walk in the boots, how could I ski? I looked over at Peter, clomping around the store in boots just like mine. He stopped and grinned at me. I tried to grin back, but I think I scowled instead.

After that, the lady brought over skis and poles. She placed a black helmet on my head and adjusted the chin straps. Next, she placed goggles over my eyes. Everything turned dark. My parents told me to put on my jacket and ski mittens. I felt so bundled up, it reminded me of this Egyptian mummy I saw once in the Museum of Natural History. The museum lady told us it was a real dead person wrapped in strips of white cloth! My whole body shuddered just thinking about it.

After everybody got their ski equipment, my parents helped me carry my stuff to the ski school. I had to walk there in those clunky boots in the snow. I kept slipping, and it felt like there were a ton of rocks in my boots. All I wanted to do was go back to bed and hide. Peter clomped over to me.

"These boots feel terrible," I said.

"Don't worry. My parents said skiing's a lot easier than walking."

I sure hoped Peter's parents were right.

CHAPTER 12

HANDSOME HANS

My dad told the ski instructors we were beginners. The instructors pointed to a pole with a giant number one on top.

"Good luck," said my dad, when we got to the pole. I'd need more than luck to survive this day, I thought.

"You'll do fine," said my mom. "Don't worry."

She might as well have told birds not to fly.

"We'll pick you up after your lesson," said Mr. Cavelli.

If we're still alive, I thought.

"Bye," said Mrs. Cavelli. Then, they left.

More kids came over to our group. They looked like five-year-olds. We watched some older kids skiing down the hill. An instructor at the bottom pointed to poles with numbers two, three, four, and five on them. The better skiers went to the higher numbers. Nobody else came to number one.

Suddenly, Peter pointed to two girls standing by pole number five.

"Hey, isn't that Lisa and Deena?"

Sure enough, I saw Lisa and Deena wearing fancy pink, turquoise, and white outfits. The expensive kind I'd seen in the store with my mom.

"Whoa, and there's Bobby and Tommy," said Peter. "I guess their parents made them take lessons after all."

Bobby and Tommy stood by the pole that said *Snowboards*. Bobby had a red and black snowboard with racing stripes on it. Tommy had a black one with white skeletons.

I slunk down into my jacket like a turtle hiding in its shell. I didn't want them to see us at pole number one with the little kids.

Once all the kids got placed into groups, an instructor skied over to us. He was cute and tall with a very tan face.

"Hi, my name is Hans," he said, smiling. "How's everybody doing today?"

A few kids nodded and said okay. Hans asked us our names and ages.

All the kids said five or six.

Peter didn't seem to care. "Peter, eight!" he shouted.

"Samantha, eight," I whispered.

"Hi Samantha," Hans said. "Don't look so scared. You're going to do great!"

I smiled and couldn't take my eyes off him.

Peter looked at Hans and me. "I already told you you'll do great, Samantha," he said, sounding annoyed.

Hans showed us how to put on our skis. He told us to lift up one boot and tap off the snow with our pole. Then click the boot into our ski.

Tap, tap, click. Tap, tap, click. Both his boots clicked into his skis. He made it look so easy.

The five and six-year-olds had no problem. Even Peter did fine. If they could do it, so could I. Right?

As soon as I lifted my foot to tap off the snow, I started to wobble. I lost my balance and ended up falling right on my butt!

The little kid named Brad laughed at me. I tried to get up but fell back down. My jeans got cold and wet.

"Shh," Hans said to Brad. He looked at me and smiled. "That happened to me the first time, too. No problem, Samantha." He came over and helped

50

me up. He let me hold onto his arm while I tapped my boot and clicked my foot into the ski. I held on and did my other foot.

"Awesome," said Hans, smiling and winking at me. I think I fell in love with him right then and there. I bet my face turned bright red, but not from the cold. Peter gave Hans a dirty look.

"Now we'll learn how to sidestep up the mountain," Hans said. "Watch."

He stood sideways, lifted one ski up the hill, and dug in the edge. Next, he moved the other ski up to meet it. He did it twice more and sure enough he got partway up the hill.

Hans skied back down and stood behind me.

"Watch again," he said. "Samantha, show them how it's done."

Me? He held onto my waist while I lifted up my ski and dug it into the hill.

"Now shift your weight up," he said.

I did.

"Now bring your other ski up."

It sounded scary but I did it anyway. Wow, it worked.

I did it twice more before I realized he'd let go of my waist! Skiing wasn't so bad after all, I thought.

The rest of the group inched up the hill.

I hoped that would be the end of the lesson and we could go inside and get hot chocolate.

Unfortunately, Hans had other ideas.

CHAPTER 13

WOBBLE AND SLIDE

Next, Hans taught us the snowplow. Which didn't mean we used a machine to push snow around. It just meant making our skis look like pizzas.

He turned his body until he faced straight down the mountain. He kept the back of his skis far apart and the tips close, making a triangle. It looked just like the pizza slice I'd seen in the book at the library.

"You won't slide forward when you make a large slice of pizza," Hans said. "But when you want to move, you make the slice smaller."

He brought his skis closer together and slid down the hill. Then, he made a bigger pizza slice, slowed down, and stopped.

"Come on Samantha, you go first," he said.

Why did I have to go first? I tried to do what he showed us, but as soon as my skis pointed downhill, I started to slide.

"Oh no!" I yelled. My body tensed and down I went back onto my butt in the snow.

More giggles from Bratty Brad and the other kids. My jeans got wetter and colder. I just wanted to give up and go inside the warm, safe lodge.

Hans sidestepped up and lifted me off the ground. He gave the kids a dirty look. He didn't let go while I made a pizza with my skis and faced downhill.

"Dig your inside edges in," he said. "That way you won't slide."

I did and sure enough, I stayed put. He skied down below me.

"Okay, now bring the back of your skis closer together, slide, and make them wide again."

My legs started to tremble.

"Come on, you can do it."

I moved my skis together a little and felt myself slide. I made a big wide pizza right away and dug my inside edges in. I stopped. I guess I did have some control. I did it again and by the third time, I ended up right by Hans. He gave me a high five and smiled.

"Awesome," he said. "You're a natural."

Peter gave Hans another dirty look. He came down next, followed by everyone else. Nobody fell.

We sidestepped back up and did it twice more.

"You guys are amazing!" said Hans.

I thought we'd learned a lot and hoped Hans would take us in for that hot chocolate, but no such luck. Instead, he taught us how to turn.

"When you want to turn left, put your weight on your right ski. To turn right, put your weight on your left ski."

Right ski, left ski, it all sounded so confusing.

"Try it, Samantha," he said.

"Brad can go first," I said.

Brad grinned and got into position. He turned right, shifted his weight and turned left.

"Excellent," said Hans.

Now that Bratty Brad had done so well, I didn't want to go at all. Peter went next and then everybody else. No one fell.

Now the pressure was on. My legs shook, and my heart beat fast.

I started to shift my weight and sure enough, I turned right. But then I started to go faster and forgot what to do next.

"Shift your weight right," said Hans.

I tried but it was like my skis had a mind of their own. I kept going right. My skis slid out in front of me, and I landed hard on the ground.

This time I didn't want to get up.

"Okay, everybody," said Hans. "Now's a good time to teach you how to get up without help. Samantha will demonstrate."

I wished he'd just leave me alone and ski off with the rest of the class. Instead, he came over and explained how to get up.

It took me three tries before succeeding.

"Now everybody, drop down to the ground and practice getting up," said Hans.

Brad started to complain so Hans just lifted him up and placed him flat on his back on the ground.

"What'd you do that for?" Brad yelled.

"So you can learn how to get up when you fall."

"But I'm not gonna fall," said Brad. "I'm not a klutz like Samantha."

"Then how come you're on the ground?" asked Hans.

The other kids giggled.

Everybody practiced falling and getting up. Then, we did some more snowplow turns. This time, I remembered to shift my weight and I turned without a problem.

"Okay," said Hans. "You guys are so good, we're going to the top of the hill on the rope tow."

CHAPTER 14

TUG AND FALL

Hans took us over to the tow.

"Stand next to the moving rope, grab onto it and let it pull you up the hill. Let go when you get to the top."

It sure beat sidestepping, I thought,

He let the little kids go first. Hans stood beside them and helped them into position. They each grabbed the rope and up they went.

Peter went next and finally it was my turn. Hans smiled at me.

"Okay Samantha. You can do it!"

Something told me it wouldn't be so easy.

I got into position and grabbed the rope. I guess I didn't expect it to pull me so hard. It jolted me forward and off balance. Down I went with the rope dragging me along in the snow.

"Let go!" yelled Hans.

I did, but it was too late. I ended up in a jumble.

The rope tow stopped moving and the kids groaned. I wanted to dig a hole in the snow, hibernate like a bear, and never come out. Skiing had to be the hardest job in the universe. Even harder than running for class president.

"Okay, slide over and get up like I showed you before," said Hans.

I slid over. Suddenly two heads appeared next to Hans. Oh no. It was Lisa and Deena.

"Hi Samantha. I thought that was you." said Lisa, smirking. "Looks like your lessons aren't going so well."

"Wow, you're all tangled up," said Deena. "And this is just the bunny hill!"

"Okay girls," said Hans. "Let's give Samantha some space. Your instructor's waiting for you downhill."

Lisa and Deena giggled some more, then skied off. They made graceful arcs from side to side. They even made French fry turns instead of pizzas. I knew I'd never get that good.

Hans looked down at me. "Are you going to let those two mean girls show you up? This is your first time skiing and you're doing great. Come on!"

Maybe it was because Hans was so cute. Or maybe because he wasn't going away until I got up. Or maybe because he looked at me like he really believed I could do it. I decided to try. First, I had to get my skis sideways to the mountain. Next, I got up like Hans taught me.

Hans made me go back to the rope tow and stood right behind me. We grabbed the rope together and it pulled us all the way uphill. When we got to the top, Hans told me to let go. I did and we skied over to the rest of the class.

"It's about time," said Brad. "Slow Poke!"

"Okay guys," said Hans, glaring at Brad. "Follow behind me and stay in my tracks."

He skied off making big wide snowplow turns and we all followed. Even me. I didn't follow his tracks exactly but I didn't fall either.

"Great!" said Hans, when we came to a stop halfway down the slope. "Let's do it again." He winked at me and I blushed like a big red tomato.

Hans skied down and we all followed. I started off great and even stayed in the tracks. I felt so good I made smaller pizzas and skied even faster. Faster and faster. It was so much fun, I guess I didn't notice Peter making big slow pizza turns in front of me. Oh no! I tried to slow down, but it was too late. Crash! I smacked into Peter and my skis went flying. My butt hit the ground and Peter and I rolled downhill in a big jumble. Finally, we stopped. Right in front of Bratty Brad!

"Wooo," said Brad, pointing and hooting. "Look at the lovebirds!"

Peter and I tried to get untangled but our skis got in the way. Hans skied over and helped us up.

"Are you two okay?" he asked.

I couldn't tell because my butt and legs had turned numb from the cold. I brushed off the snow from the back of my jeans. That's when things got even worse.

"Oh look. Samantha wet her pants," yelled Brad. "Samantha Wet-Her-Pants!"

"Samantha Wet-Her-Pants!" repeated the kids.

"Enough!" yelled Hans, shaking his head. "It's time to go inside for a hot chocolate break."

I think those were the best words I'd heard in my entire life.

CHAPTER 15

HOT AND COLD

We snowplowed down to the bottom of the mountain. When we arrived, we took off our skis and placed them on wooden racks. Then, we trudged into the lodge clunking our boots like a herd of elephants in tap shoes. Hans found us a table and made us sit down while he got hot chocolates.

I sat but I still couldn't feel my butt. I once read about a girl who got frostbite and lost her finger. I wondered if I'd get frostbite too and my whole butt would fall off. I asked Peter about it. He said I should tell Hans. I shook my head. I didn't want to talk to Hans about my butt falling off!

Hans came back with a tray of hot chocolates and passed them out. I saw Peter whisper in his ear. Oh no, I thought. Hans came right over to me.

"Why don't you sit by the fire, so you can warm up." He pointed to a couch in front of a crackling fire. "I'll come get you when we're ready to leave."

"I'm not going back," I said.

"Why not, Samantha? You're getting the hang of it. Falling is part of the learning process."

"No, I'm done."

I took my hot chocolate and trudged over to the fireplace. Peter joined me. I think I heard Brad call us *lovebirds* but I didn't care. I made up my mind never to ski again.

The fire felt warm and toasty and I started to thaw out. After a few minutes, Hans walked over.

"What do you say Samantha? Will you try again?"

"Nope." I shook my head.

"Well I'm sorry to hear that. But I'll have to call your parents to let them know where you are."

I didn't want Hans to call, but I didn't want to ski either.

"I'll stay with Samantha," said Peter.

"No Peter," said Hans. "You should go back out skiing. Your parents paid for your lesson."

Hans took out his cell phone, tapped in a number, and spoke into the phone. A few minutes later, my parents came into the lodge.

They talked to Hans and came over to me. Hans and the class filed out. Peter waved to me right before he left. That's when I started to cry.

"Hey Samantha," said my mom. "It's my fault. We should have bought you ski pants earlier. Everybody falls when they first learn and jeans get icy cold. How about we go back to the motel and get you some warm clothes? We'll come back later to buy ski pants at the store."

"I don't need ski pants because I'm never skiing again."

"Why not? Hans told me you did great."

"He's lying."

"I don't think so."

"Come on," said my Dad. "We'll talk about it later. For now, let's just get you warmed up."

We got my shoes from the locker and my skis from outside. It felt so good to get out of those clunky boots. When we got to the motel, I changed into warm clothes. What a relief!

CHAPTER 16

SKI SHOCK

After I warmed up, we drove back to the mountain and went into the lodge.

"You go skiing," my mom told my dad. "I'll shop for ski pants with Samantha."

"No," I said. "You might as well save your money." I crossed my arms and stood my ground.

My mom nodded to my dad. He shrugged and left the lodge.

"Okay," she said. "I'll just browse in the shop awhile. Why don't you sit by the window and relax." Off she went.

The window stretched from floor to ceiling. Through it, I could see hundreds of skiers sashaying down the slope. It looked a lot steeper than the bunny hill, but everybody looked happy. That made me feel even worse. I started to turn away when suddenly I spotted something strange. A kid flew down the mountain sitting in a chair with skis attached to the bottom. I couldn't believe my eyes.

I rushed outside to get a better look. The kid in the chair leaned side to side and the chair turned right and left. She had poles attached to her wrists with ski tips on the ends. It looked like someone had chopped off the back of the skis and just left the tips. A man skied behind her holding straps attached to the chair. He pulled back to slow it down. Even so, the chair sped all the way to the bottom of the hill.

A woman next to me started clapping. I turned to look.

"Go Sophia!" she yelled. "You're awesome."

Sophia? That was the name of the new girl in my class. Could it be?

My mom came running out of the lodge.

"Samantha," she said. "I got worried when I didn't find you by the window. You shouldn't wander off like that...Oh Mrs. Lin, how are you?"

I turned to the girl in the chair. The instructor removed her helmet and sure enough there was Sophia, smiling with one side of her mouth. Her eyes sparkled. The whole thing left me speechless.

My mom and Mrs. Lin talked for a while. Mrs. Lin called the special ski chair, *bi-skis*, and the poles with ski tips, *outriggers*. By leaning side to side and using the outriggers, Sophia could ski even though she couldn't walk.

Sophia made a few muffled sounds but I couldn't understand her. She didn't have her iPad. After a while, we said goodbye and walked back into the lodge.

"So," my mom said. "Now that you've seen Sophia skiing, don't you think you should try again?"

I didn't answer. She led me straight to the ski shop and I followed. I don't even remember trying anything on, but somehow we left with a brand new pair of black waterproof pants in just the right size. My mom kept muttering about highway robbery. Which didn't mean, we were out on the road getting our money stolen. It just meant she thought she paid way too much money for my pants.

CHAPTER 17

WORDS OF WISDOM

After my dad finished skiing, we drove back to the motel. My mom told him all about Sophia's special ski chair.

"What do you think of that?" asked my dad.

I shrugged. I guessed they thought Sophia was brave and I was just a scaredy cat. But Sophia got to sit down and have an instructor hold onto her chair so she wouldn't fall. That had to be easier than doing it on your own.

After that, my mom made dinner reservations.

"Nine people at 6:30," she said into her phone.

"Nine?" I asked, when she hung up.

"Yes. We're having dinner with the Cavellis and the Lins at Snuggler's Cove."

"I thought we had discount coupons for Black Diamond Pizza."

"We did, but they don't have a ramp for wheelchairs so we had to change restaurants."

Just when I thought Sophia had it easier, it turns out she didn't. She could only eat in restaurants with wheelchair access.

After I showered and dressed, I checked my Kindle. It had completely charged. I downloaded *Anne of Green Gables* and started reading. I could make the fonts bigger or smaller and bookmark my pages. If I highlighted a word I didn't know, the definition came right up on the screen. When I swiped my finger across the screen, the page turned. I could even go backwards. Reading on the Kindle was so much fun, I almost forgot about my lousy day.

"Okay, let's go," said my dad, interrupting me.

"Just a couple more minutes, please?" I asked.

"Nope," said my dad. "We don't want to be late."

When we got to the restaurant, the Cavellis had already arrived. We joined them at the table. Soon, I spotted Sophia steering her wheelchair towards us with her parents walking behind.

"Hi Samantha. Hi Peter," said Sophia's iPad voice. She had her iPad on her tray.

"Hi," we said.

"Wasn't skiing great?" she asked.

"Awesome!" said Peter. Then he looked at me. "Samantha did great, too. You're skiing tomorrow, aren't you?"

"I don't want to," I said

"Why not?" asked Sophia.

"Because I keep falling and all the bratty little kids in our class laugh at me."

"Ignore them," said Sophia. "That's what I do."

I guessed kids made fun of Sophia a lot.

A waitress came over and asked for our drink orders. Peter and I asked for hot chocolates.

"Water," said Sophia. The waitress looked around confused.

"Sophia will have water," said Mrs. Lin, pointing to her daughter. "With a straw."

"Oh...okay," said the waitress. Then she handed everybody menus except for Sophia.

"What about me?" asked Sophia.

The waitress looked startled. She looked at Sophia's iPad. "Oh, does that thing talk for you?"

"Yes," said Sophia. "Can I have a menu?"

"Oh, hmm. I didn't think you could read."

"Of course she can!" said Mrs. Lin.

"Oh, I'm so sorry," said the waitress. "I didn't mean...I mean...oh...here's a menu." She placed a menu on Sophia's tray and hurried off.

"See," said Sophia. "People assume I'm stupid. I don't let it upset me."

Sophia opened the menu with her right hand and dropped her left one on top to keep it open. Her mom tilted her head down so she could see it. Even reading a menu was hard for Sophia, but she didn't complain.

"Have you decided what you want?" asked Mrs. Cavelli.

"I'll have spaghetti," said Peter. "With meatballs and cheese."

"Me too," I said.

"Me three," said Sophia.

Mrs. Lin frowned. "Are you sure?"

"Sure," said Sophia.

When the waitress returned with our drinks, Sophia sipped through her straw while Peter and I drank our hot chocolates. Peter asked Sophia how her ski chair worked and she told him all about it.

"I want to race one day," said Sophia. "But first I have to get good enough to ski without a teacher."

"Aren't you scared?" I asked.

"Why?" asked Sophia.

"Because you might fall out of your chair and break something," I said.

"You shouldn't let your fear of falling stop you from skiing, Samantha. I love the rush of cold air on my face and speeding down the mountain. It doesn't feel like I have a disability when I ski."

Sophia clicked her iPad so fast to get out all those words. I figured she liked speed typing as much as she liked speed skiing.

"Maybe I can learn to race too!" said Peter.

I looked back and forth between Peter and Sophia. "Well, I don't see what's so fun. It's cold and wet and everything feels so heavy. I'd rather just read a good book."

It seemed like neither of them heard me.

"How do you get your ski chair on the lift?" Peter asked her.

Tap, tap, tap. She answered immediately, but I stopped listening. I wondered if Peter liked Sophia more than he liked me.

CHAPTER 18

MORE WORDS OF WISDOM

Our dinner finally arrived.

"My mom showed me how to roll spaghetti around my fork," said Peter.

He rolled some spaghetti and raised it to his mouth. He took a big bite, but some of the spaghetti and sauce slid down his chin. I laughed and Sophia half-smiled.

I went next. I twirled the fork around and around so I wouldn't make a mess like Peter. I got most of it in my mouth except for one noodle which I slurped in fast. Drops of sauce flew to the other side of the table and splattered Sophia.

"Oops," I said, wiping my mouth with my napkin. But Sophia just kept half-smiling.

"My turn," she typed on her iPad.

Sophia tried to twirl the spaghetti but it kept sliding off. After the third try, she just picked some up and stuffed it in her mouth.

Peter and I gasped. Sauce and noodles dripped down Sophia's chin. She wiped her face with a napkin.

"Delicious," she typed on her iPad with a tomato smeared hand.

"Best way to eat it!" said Peter. He picked up a clump of spaghetti and shoved it in his mouth. Sophia made funny gasping sounds and had that sparkle in her eyes again.

Why not? I thought. I grabbed some spaghetti and shoved it in my mouth too. When I looked up, I saw our parents staring at us, dumbstruck. Which didn't mean they turned stupid. It just meant they couldn't believe their eyes.

"What about your manners?" asked Mrs.Cavelli.

"We're in a restaurant," said my mom.

Everybody got quiet.

"Well, spaghetti's a messy meal," said Mrs. Lin, finally breaking the silence. "Bon appetite!"

"That's French for have a good meal," typed Sophia. Wow, Sophia knew French too.

After a couple of awkward seconds, the rest of the grownups said, "Bon appetite!"

So we finished our spaghetti with slurps and shoves and a big tomato sauce mess. I think it was the most fun meal in the entire galaxy.

When the waitress came over and saw what we'd done, she gasped and ran off. She returned with a sponge and wet-naps. The wet-naps came in little foil packets that Peter and I ripped open. Inside, we found folded napkins wet with soap.

"Let me open it for you," said Peter when he saw Sophia struggling. Sophia smiled.

Hmm, I thought. Maybe they're falling in love.

We wiped our hands and faces while the waitress cleaned the table.

"Would you like any dessert?" she asked when she finished. "We have chocolate cake, ice cream, and jell-o."

"Jell-o," typed Sophia.

"No way!" said all the grownups at the same time. I guess they thought we'd make another mess. So instead we had ice cream sodas that we slurped through straws.

Right before we left the restaurant, Sophia typed me a message.

"I really hope you ski tomorrow."

"I don't think so," I said.

"Don't give up," she typed.

"It's too hard."

"Everything I do is hard. If you really want to ski badly enough, you will. It just takes practice."

"But everybody keeps laughing at me."

"Kids make fun of me all the time. They stare and call me names. Especially when I drool. Ignore them."

I nodded.

"And one more thing," she typed. "Let people help you." Sophia's eyes moved toward Peter.

"But, I like to do things myself," I said.

"I do too, but sometimes I just can't."

"Thanks," I said.

I didn't know if I'd ski the next day or not, but Sophia got me to thinking. I decided to sleep on it. Which didn't mean I'd put skis in my bed and lie on top of them. It just meant, I'd wait until morning to decide.

CHAPTER 19

DOWN AND OUT

The next day, my parents woke me early. My legs felt achy, and I just wanted to stay in bed with my Kindle. No such luck. My mom made me get up, brush my teeth, and get dressed.

The motel served rolls, donuts, cereal, and juice for breakfast. After we ate, we drove to the slopes. Before I knew it, I had on my clunky boots and was carrying my skis to the number one sign on the bunny slope. When I arrived, Hans' face lit up.

"Welcome back, Samantha. I like your new pants."

I blushed.

"Oh no, look who's back," said Bratty Brad.

"Boooo," said another kid.

I remembered what Sophia said and just ignored them. I felt better when Peter showed up. We all clicked into our skis.

"Okay," said Hans. "We'll start on the Moon Beam chairlift. Follow me."

Uh oh, I thought. A chairlift?

Hans skied off. I copied the kids skating my skis side to side to move forward on the flat snow. It was hard and I ended up arriving last.

"Samantha Slow Poke!" said Brad.

"Bratty Brad!" Peter said.

Kids giggled.

"Okay, who remembers how to get on the lift?" asked Hans.

Everybody raised their hands except me.

"Peter, why don't you explain it to Samantha."

Peter beamed and explained what to do.

"Perfect," said Hans. "Samantha, you come with me." I blushed again.

We entered the ski school line. When the chair passed by for the people in front of us, we moved into position. I turned my head backwards and the ski operator slowed down the chair. I grabbed the side and sat down. Presto! Just like that I got on. Hans lowered the safety bar in front of us. Then, we lifted our skis and set them on the footrest.

"Not so bad, right Samantha?" asked Hans.

"Right," I said, feeling proud of myself.

We rode the chair up the slope when suddenly I panicked.

"Uh, oh," I said. "How do I get off?"

"Easy," said Hans. He explained what to do. It sounded really hard, but Hans lifted the safety bar and told me when to scoot forward on my chair. I stood up, skied down a hill, and turned left. Easy.

We waited for the rest of the kids to come up the lift.

"Slow Poke!" I said to Brad who was the last to arrive.

Peter clapped.

Hans led us down the slope. It was steeper than the bunny hill, but I made the turns easily. I couldn't believe how much I remembered.

"Great job!" said Hans.

We skied back to the lift and did it again. The turns got even easier and I didn't fall at all.

Hans taught us how to stop quicker and keep our skis more parallel. We skied down steeper trails. The sun shone and the snow glistened. Hans even let me ski at the front of the class. We stopped halfway down a trail called Uh Oh Run. That's when we spotted Sophia speeding down the mountain in her chair.

"Wow!" said Brad. "That's cool."

Peter and I smiled. Sophia would love to hear someone calling her cool.

Right behind Sophia, I saw Lisa and Deena skiing with their class. I watched them carve quick turns, keeping their skis close together. They stopped right next to me and laughed.

"What's so funny?" I asked.

"You got left back," said Lisa.

"I'm still in third grade like you," I said.

"No, dummy, your ski class left you back!"

I turned around and sure enough Hans and the class had already skied on. I tried to catch up. I made smaller turns so I could ski faster. I almost reached them, when suddenly I heard a big whooping sound behind me. I turned and my skis followed my head to the right.

"Look out!" screamed a snowboarder, hot-dogging down the mountain. I tried to get out of the way, but my tips crossed and I fell over. Crash! When the snowboarder smacked into me, he felt like a giant rock. I tumbled down the mountain. My skis came off and my legs got twisted underneath me. I put my foot out to stop myself from rolling and felt my ankle wrench. Ouch! I finally stopped and the snowboarder crashed into me again. I recognized him right away. Bobby Stanger!

CHAPTER 20

LIMPING HOME

Before I knew it, dozens of faces stared down at me.

"Are you okay?" someone asked. "Can you stand up?"

"She's fine," said another voice. It sounded like Lisa Logan. "She's just looking for attention. Come on, get up. You too Bobby."

I tried to get up but my leg buckled under me. Suddenly, handsome Hans appeared over me like an angel from heaven.

"Stay down. Ski patrol's on its way," he said.

Four men in red jackets with white crosses pushed through the crowd. They lifted Bobby and me onto stretchers mounted on sleds. They buckled us in and pulled us down the mountain.

They carried me into a big room that smelled like medicine and transferred me onto a bed. Seconds later, they brought in Bobby and set him next to me. I wanted to yell at him for crashing into me, but I didn't because his body was shaking and he started crying, "Mommy, mommy."

After that, things happened so fast, it all seemed like a blur. A nurse checked my leg and covered it with an ice pack. The cold felt good and eased the pain. My parents showed up. They fussed over me and spoke to the nurse. Then they drove me to a hospital where doctors looked at my leg and took x-rays. They told my parents I was lucky, it was only an ankle fracture. The other boy had a broken leg. Poor Bobby. My parents got me crutches and pain medicine. We rode to the motel, packed up, and drove to the mountain to return our skis. I waited in the car.

My parents returned with a whole bunch of people following them. Bratty Brad, Handsome Hans, Peter, Lisa, Deena, and Tommy.

"Everybody wanted to see how you were doing," said my mom.

"Can we see your crutches?" asked Bratty Brad.

"Is your leg broken?" asked Deena.

"Does it hurt?" asked Peter.

"How's Bobby doing?" asked Tommy.

"I'm so sorry you got hurt Samantha," said Hans. "You were skiing so well. I hope you get better and come back soon."

I got really popular, but I felt so sleepy, it didn't seem to matter. The last thing I remembered was Lisa glaring at me, her arms folded.

"Come on everybody," she said. "Let's go back and ski. No point in wasting the day here!"

CHAPTER 21

VISITING HOURS

Back home, I rested and read lots of books on my Kindle. I iced my ankle and kept it up on a pillow. When I got up, I put on a black boot that kept my ankle straight. At first, walking on crutches hurt my underarms but my mom wrapped the top with soft cloths. Once I got the hang of it, I could move really fast.

A couple of days later, the Cavelli and Lin families came over to visit. Sophia's dad had to carry her into the house while my dad brought in her wheelchair. That's because we didn't have a ramp for our front steps.

"How was skiing?" I asked.

"Great!" Sophia typed. "I even skied without my instructor."

"You should have seen her, Samantha," said Peter. He looked at Sophia and beamed with pride. "She did great. Everybody stopped to watch."

"Cool," I said, wondering if Peter really had fallen in love with Sophia.

"How about you, Peter? Did you have fun?"

Peter must have seen my sad face, because he hesitated before answering. "It wasn't as much fun without you. Everybody talked about you and Bobby and the accident. Even Bratty Brad. And Hans said to get better soon."

That made me smile.

We decided to play a game. We tried playing Spit. Sophia couldn't throw her cards out fast enough so we played rummy instead.

Then, Peter tried walking with my crutches. He wobbled and almost fell.

"You'd better get a wheelchair," typed Sophia. "You're not good on crutches!"

Peter just laughed. We decided to tell jokes.

"Why did the crayon run away crying?" Sophia typed.

"Why?" we asked.

"Because it was blue!"

It wasn't that funny, but we laughed anyway.

"What did the math class use instead of desks?" asked Peter.

"What?" we asked.

"Times tables!"

We laughed some more.

"How do you get straight A's?" I asked.

"How?"

"Using a ruler!" I said.

The sillier the joke the more fun we had. By the time they left, I didn't feel jealous anymore. I realized I was the luckiest girl on the planet to have two great friends instead of just one.

CHAPTER 22

CRUTCHES AND ELEVATORS

After the holiday break, my mom drove me back to school. Peter helped me carry my books. By that time, I could move really fast on crutches. Kids gathered around me and took turns trying them out.

Then Bobby came in with Tommy. Instead of a black boot like mine, he had a big white cast. Kids lined up to sign their names on it and the whole room buzzed with excitement. Ms. Thompson had to ask us three times to quiet down.

When Lisa and Deena came in late, I couldn't believe my eyes. Lisa had crutches too! She had an ace bandage wrapped around her ankle.

"What happened to you?" asked Stacey Spiros.

"I twisted my ankle skiing," she said. "I jumped off a gigantic mogul on a triple black diamond run and landed wrong."

I knew black diamond runs were for experts, but I'd never heard of a triple black one.

"Wow!" said Jenny Becker. "Look at your crutches. They are way cool."

Sure enough, the underarm rests and handholds had zebra print fabric with pink polka dots.

"All right, everybody," said Ms. Thompson. "Let's sit down and get to work." She moved some extra chairs near the three of us so we could rest our legs. She placed our crutches in the corner of the room.

At ten o'clock, we went to gym. Lisa, Bobby, and I rode in the elevator with Sophia and Mrs. Sparkle instead of taking the stairs.

"Hey, this is so cool," said Bobby.

"Whatever," said Lisa.

"Hey, now we're just like you, Sophia," I said. "We're taking the elevator because we all have disabilities."

"Not exactly," typed Sophia. "You guys will get better and walk again, but I'll always use a wheelchair. It's okay, though. It's just how I get around."

"Ohh," I said. I hadn't thought about it like that. I guessed it was kind of like me wearing glasses in order to see clearly. We all had different things we used to help us. If Sophia was okay with that, then I should be too.

CHAPTER 23

RACE TO THE FINISH

In gym, Bobby and I handed Mr. Spalding our doctors' notes. Lisa said she forgot to bring hers.

"Bring it tomorrow," he said, excusing her from gym anyway.

We sat on the floor next to Sophia. She always got excused from gym. Mrs. Sparkle helped her do exercises like squeezing a ball and lifting weights.

"This stinks," Bobby said, watching the class do relay races. "I'm bored!"

"I'm not," said Lisa. She filed her nails and painted hot pink nail polish on them.

"Hey, I've got an idea," Sophia typed. "You guys should have a race."

"Huh?" I asked. "We can't even walk."

"That's right," she typed. "You can race with your crutches."

Bobby's face lit up. "Hey, that's a great idea. A crutch race." He looked me right in the eye. "You don't have a chance against me, Samantha!"

"Oh yeah," I said, remembering how fast I'd gotten. "I bet I can beat you!" Oops, now why did I say that? Bobby always beat everybody.

"What about you Lisa?" typed Sophia.

"My nails have to dry," she said.

"Scaredy cat," said Bobby.

"Am not!" yelled Lisa.

"Are so!" yelled Bobby.

"Hey what's going on here?" asked Mr. Spalding, rushing over.

Mrs. Sparkle told Mr. Spalding about the race. I thought he'd say no way, but he surprised me.

"Great idea!" he said, turning to the class. "Okay everybody, let's make room so Bobby, Lisa, and Samantha can race."

The kids cheered. Mr. Spalding set up the starting line at one end of the gym.

"Go to the other side, touch the wall with your crutch, and come back."

He walked over to Sophia and handed her a whistle. "It was your idea," he said, "so you can be the referee." Sophia's eyes lit up.

Bobby, Lisa, and I lined up. Everybody gathered on the sideline, cheering and hooting. The girls rooted for Lisa and the boys rooted for Tommy, but Peter shouted the loudest of all. "Go Samantha!"

Sophia blew the whistle and off we went. Bobby shot ahead of me. He had longer crutches and took bigger strides. I made steady progress while Lisa wobbled behind. I tried hard to catch up to Bobby by planting my crutches further in front of me and swinging my legs all the way through but Bobby kept the lead. Lisa fell further behind.

Bobby reached the wall first and hopped around. All of a sudden, Lisa passed me by. What? How'd that happen? That's when I saw it. Lisa had stopped hopping and ran with both feet on the ground!

Screech! Sophia blew the whistle and everybody froze.

"Lisa cheated," she typed. "She faked a sprained ankle."

Everybody glared at Lisa.

"Well, it started to feel better," she said. "So I put some weight on it. Nobody said I had to hop."

"Booo!" yelled Stacey.

"Cheater!" yelled Kevin.

"You're disqualified!" typed Sophia.

"Well I didn't want to race in the first place," Lisa said. "It was your stupid idea."

"Sit down, Lisa," said Mr. Spalding. "I'll talk with you later. In the meantime, we'll have to start again, without Lisa."

Bobby and I lined up. Now that Lisa was disqualified, all the girls rooted for me. That made me want to beat Bobby even more.

Sophia blew the whistle and Bobby shot out in front. I pulled hard and hopped forward. Bobby kept the lead but I wasn't far behind. I touched the wall just a couple of seconds after him and turned to face the finish line. Bobby zoomed off like a high-speed locomotive.

"Come on Samantha, you can do it!" I heard.

That's when I remembered what Sophia told me. *If you really want something badly enough, you can do it.* I decided right then and there to pull out all the stops. I reached further forward and pulled harder and faster than ever. I swung my whole body through. Again and again, faster and faster. My arms ached, but I kept going. Only one stride behind Bobby.

"Come on Samantha, you can do it! Go, go, go!"

Suddenly Bobby slowed down. He must have tired out, but I still had lots of energy. I pulled and swung like a robot on auto-pilot, focusing all my attention on the goal. A surge of energy shot through me. I closed my eyes and dashed for the finish line. I don't remember what happened next but when I opened my eyes, we had reached the wall.

Kids cheered. Oh well, I thought. I tried my best.

"Great race, you guys," said Mr. Spalding. "Congratulations Samantha!" He shook my hand.

"Huh?" I asked.

"You won," typed Sophia.

I couldn't believe it. I actually beat Bobby, the fastest kid in the galaxy. Kids rushed in and fist bumped me. So that's what being popular feels like, I thought.

I saw Bobby and Tommy slinking away from the crowd. Bobby hung his head and Tommy patted him on the back. I hopped over to them.

"Good race," I said, holding out my hand to Bobby. "You had me beat the whole way."

Bobby hesitated before shaking my hand.

"Thanks," he said, but he still looked sad.

"Hey, do you want to have a rematch tomorrow?" I asked.

His face suddenly lit up.

"You're on!" he said.

CHAPTER 24

TWO SMARTYPANTS

After the race, Mr. Spalding spoke to Lisa about good sportsmanship. She glared at me and Bobby. She didn't even bother with the crutches anymore now that the cat was out of the bag. Which didn't mean a pet got loose in the gym. It just meant everyone knew her secret. We rode the elevator down without her.

"I hope you both get better and we all go back to Devil's Drop," typed Sophia.

"Me too," said Bobby.

"Me three!" I said, surprising myself. Only a week before, skiing had terrified me.

"By the way, thanks Samantha," said Bobby.

"For what?" I asked.

"For not ratting me out about crying when I broke my leg," he whispered.

"You cried?" I asked, pretending I hadn't seen him. He grinned.

I turned to Sophia.

"And thank you, Sophia," I said.

"For what?" she typed.

"For telling me I could do anything if I wanted it badly enough," I said. "That was smart."

"Oh, that," she typed.

"I guess you really are Sophia Smartypants after all," said Bobby.

"Actually, I think Samantha and I are sisters," typed Sophia. "You can call us Samantha and Sophia Smartypants."

I grinned. I think that made me feel even happier than winning the race.

Book Discussion Questions

1) Do you get scared when you try something new? What kinds of activities scare you? What can you do to fight your fear?

2) Have you ever met anyone with cerebral palsy? What were your reactions when you first met them? How did your reactions change over time?

3) Have you ever gotten teased by your schoolmates? How did you handle it?

4) How do you react when you get a gift you don't like? What is the best thing to say?

5) Have you ever tried to do something and you kept failing at it? Did you give up? If not, what did you do to finally master it?

6) Sophia says that you can do anything if you want it badly enough. Are there some things you won't be able to do no matter how hard you try?

7) Do you prefer to do things yourself or get help from other people? Which way is best? Why?

8) Have you ever gotten jealous when your friend paid more attention to someone else? What can you do to feel better?

Acknowledgements

With special thanks to Reggie Neal, Chief Clinical Officer at United Cerebral Palsy of Hudson County. Visit www.ucpofhudsoncounty.org for donations and to learn more about their services.

Special thanks also go to Angela D'Alessandro, M.D. Pediatric Physiatrist, and Sara Puccia, Teacher, Certified in Special Education. Your insights were invaluable.

To the greatest advance readers in the galaxy, thanks go to third-going-into-fourth-graders, Katie, Lauren, Julianna, Bridget, and Lillie for their amazing comments and suggestions.

For professional editing and their continuous support, thank you to my fellow authors, Ann Dziemianowicz and Cynthia Rositano.

To the wonderful teachers and librarians who read and critiqued this manuscript, I'm indebted to Beth Papaz, Trisha Noble, Kathleen Collins, and Maggie Suarez.

To my amazing, talented, and creative illustrator, Emma Kane. Thank you for bringing my characters so fully to life.

Finally, to the three most important people in my life, my husband Mark, and my beautiful daughters, Sara and Natalie. Thank you for all your love and support.

About the Author

Barbara Puccia has written short stories, magazine articles, and web content in addition to the Samantha Smartypants chapter books. Barbara loves reading and writing and gets to bring the joy of books into other people's lives at her job in a local library. She lives with her husband in Ramsey, New Jersey and has two grown daughters who are the pride and joy of her life.

About the Cover Illustrator

Emma Kane attends Alfred University as an Art and Design major. She enjoys drawing anything from cats to dragons and zombies. Most of her inspiration comes from such things as anime and video games along with more natural things like insects and prehistoric animals. Someday, she would like to become either a special effects makeup artist or a wildlife photographer.